S.W.I.T.C.H.

SERUM WHICH INSTIGATES TOTAL CELLULAR HIJACK

Spider Stampede

Ali Sparkes

illustrated by

Ross Collins

OXFORD

UNIVERSITY PRESS

OXFORD
UNIVERSITY PRESS

Great Clarendon Street, Oxford OX2 6DP

Oxford University Press is a department of the University of Oxford.
It furthers the University's objective of excellence in research, scholarship,
and education by publishing worldwide in

Oxford   New York

Auckland Cape Town Dar es Salaam Hong Kong Karachi
Kuala Lumpur Madrid Melbourne Mexico City Nairobi
New Delhi Shanghai Taipei Toronto

With offices in

Argentina Austria Brazil Chile Czech Republic France Greece
Guatemala Hungary Italy Japan Poland Portugal Singapore
South Korea Switzerland Thailand Turkey Ukraine Vietnam

Oxford is a registered trade mark of Oxford University Press
in the UK and in certain other countries

Text © Ali Sparkes 2011
Illustrations © Ross Collins 2011
S.W.I.T.C.H. logo designed by Dynamo Ltd

The moral rights of the author have been asserted

Database right Oxford University Press (maker)

First published 2011

British Library Cataloguing in Publication Data
Data available

ISBN: 978-0-19-2729323
1 3 5 7 9 10 8 6 4 2

Printed in Great Britain

Paper used in the production of this book is a natural,
recyclable product made from wood grown in sustainable forests.
The manufacturing process conforms to the environmental
regulations of the country of origin.

For Niall

Danny and Josh
(and Piddle)

They might be twins but they're NOT the same! Josh loves insects, spiders, beetles and bugs. Danny can't stand them. Anything little with multiple legs freaks him out. So sharing a bedroom with Josh can be . . . erm . . . interesting. Mind you, they both love putting earwigs in big sister Jenny's pants drawer . . .

Danny

- FULL NAME: Danny Phillips
- AGE: 8 years
- HEIGHT: Taller than Josh
- FAVOURITE THING: Skateboarding
- WORST THING: Creepy-crawlies and tidying
- AMBITION: To be a stunt man

Josh

- FULL NAME: Josh Phillips
- AGE: 8 years
- HEIGHT: Taller than Danny
- FAVOURITE THING: Collecting insects
- WORST THING: Skateboarding
- AMBITION: To be an entomologist

Piddle

- FULL NAME: Piddle the dog Phillips
- AGE: 2 dog years
  (14 in human years)
- HEIGHT: Not very
- FAVOURITE THING: Chasing sticks
- WORST THING: Cats
- AMBITION: To bite a squirrel

CONTENTS

Losing Piddle

'AAAAAAAARRRRRGGGGHHHHHH!!!!'

  'GETITOFF—GETITOFF—
GETITOFFMEEEE!!!!'

Josh looked up from his book to see his twin brother running round in circles by the hedge, wearing nothing but swimming trunks and a look of panic.

Oh no—not true.

He was also wearing a spider.

'DON'T just sit there!' squeaked Danny, as he whirled about. 'Get it OFF!'

Josh sighed and put his book down on the grass. It was amazing, he thought, that the spider could possibly hang on while his brother was thrashing about so wildly. It was a garden spider and quite large—probably female. It had run up Danny's arm when he went to pick up his water pistol and then scarpered over his shoulder. Josh knew this because of the kind of dance his brother had just done across the grass. A sort of backwards shimmy, with gasps of horror, followed by madly flapping arms and then the whirling as his unwelcome passenger legged it down his shoulder blade.

'You should go in for the Under Nines Disco Championship,' Josh said, as he dodged under a flailing arm to scoop up the dizzy spider, now hanging on to the waistband of Danny's trunks.

'Oh very funny!' squealed Danny. 'Have you got it? Is it gone?!'

'Yes—calm down. Look! She's a beauty!' Josh cupped the spider in his hands and held it out for Danny to see. It was nut brown with mottled yellow patterns on its back.

'NOOO! Get it away from me!'

'But look—she's got these amazing feet that can hook on to stuff while she's hanging upside down and—'

'Just STOP talking about the S-P-I-D-E-R!'

growled Danny. He shuddered and refused to look while Josh gently dropped it behind the shed.

'She'll be back over by the hedge again in no time,' said Josh, which didn't comfort his twin much. 'Along with all the others. You're never more than a few feet away from a spider, you know.'

'Not *one* more *word* to do with . . . those . . . *things*!'

Josh pushed his hands into his shorts pockets

and grinned. 'Mandibles,' he muttered, quietly. He didn't think Danny would know what this word was. He'd read only yesterday that 'mandibles' were what spiders used for eating. Not teeth exactly— just sort of munchy bits on their faces.

Danny hated anything creepy-crawly. For twins, he and Josh were very different. Josh was fascinated by small creatures and bugs. He had loads of wildlife books. He used to bring woodlice, snails, and beetles into the house, but after Jenny, their older sister, found earwigs in her hairdryer and then Danny screamed loud enough to wake the dead after stepping into his brother's box of centipedes when he got up for the toilet in the middle of the night, Mum said Josh could only look at bugs and stuff outside. It was probably just as well because if Jenny didn't squash them flat with a sandal, Mum would suck them up in the vacuum cleaner—or Piddle would eat them. Piddle, their scruffy little terrier (named after a habit he had when he got overexcited) liked nothing more than to munch up a spider if he spotted one sauntering by.

'How can you *like* those things?' Danny asked,

pulling his shorts and T-shirt on over his swimming trunks. He'd gone off the paddling pool—too many dead flies in it. 'Eeeuuw! I wish there weren't any insects in the world!'

'One—spiders aren't insects, they're arachnids,' said Josh, getting up onto the climbing frame, 'and two, if there were no insects in the world we would all die out. The human race depends on them.'

'You freaky little bug boffin!' muttered Danny.

'Lucky for you that I *do* like them!' added Josh. 'Or we'd *both* be screaming and disco-dancing all over the garden right now.'

Danny ignored him—but he checked his spiky fair hair with a shiver, just in case another spider had dropped in. Josh's hair was short and neat and he wouldn't mind a spider in it at all. How could twins be so un-alike? wondered Danny as he pulled on his trainers. He loved playing computer games and listening to loud music. Josh would rather play with newts and listen to birdsong.

But, Danny had to admit, he *was* useful for creepy-crawly removal.

Danny abandoned the water pistol and picked

up his skateboard. Soon he was pelting up and
down the path with Piddle racing along beside
him, yapping and nearly tripping him up every ten
seconds.

Upstairs, from Jenny's bedroom window, a
pop tune thumped loudly, while from the kitchen
poured the burble of daytime TV, which their mum
liked to watch while she did the ironing.

From the other side of the high wooden fence
there came a thump. And then another thump.
And then a crotchety voice. '*Will* you all shut up!
I'd have a quieter afternoon on the main runway
at Heathrow Airport!' Josh grimaced. It was Miss

Potts who lived in the run-down red-brick house next door. People thought she was a bit eccentric. An old misery more like, thought Josh.

'I SAID,' came the voice again, louder. 'Will you all SHUT UP?!'

But Mum and Jenny and Danny and Piddle were all making way too much noise to hear. 'Sorry, Miss Potts,' said Josh, feeling embarrassed. 'I'll ask them to be quieter.'

'Oh, don't bother!' she snapped back, the top of her tweedy hat the only thing he could see over the fence. 'I'll soon be deaf and then it won't matter!'

Josh made flappy 'shushing' movements at Danny and mouthed, 'Miss Potts!'

Danny skidded his skateboard to a halt, shaking his head, and Piddle sat back on his furry bottom and waited, wiggling impatiently, for the fun to start again.

Josh ran past him and pushed the kitchen window shut and at once the noise from Mum's TV programme dropped. He could still hear Miss Potts though, just on the other side of the fence.

She was muttering, 'Remember! Remember! *Oh, you stupid old biddy!* Remember! Where did you hide them? Where?'

Josh bent down and peered through a knothole in the wood and saw the old lady crawling along through the weeds, which were nearly as tall as he was, obviously searching for something. Then she suddenly bobbed up, thwacked her hand hard against her forehead and snapped: 'STUPID old woman! Had to go and get your brain burnt out, didn't you?' Then she stood up and stomped off into her ramshackle garden shed.

It was right what they said about Petty Potts, Josh decided. She really was mad.

'She's always moaning about noise,' Danny said, suddenly, in his ear. Josh jumped. 'Does she think this is a library or something? It's a blummin' garden! Kids play in gardens. Dogs play in gardens!' And he picked up a rubber ball and threw it for Piddle. 'There you go, Piddle! Catch!'

Piddle hurtled down the path and then threw himself into the heap of cuttings and compost in the far corner. 'Don't pay any attention to her—old whinge-pants,' said Danny. 'Come on, Piddle! Here, boy!'

They glanced back down the garden, expecting to see Piddle foraging through the leaves and cut grass—and then they both blinked, and stared back at each other in surprise.

Piddle had vanished.

Turning Yellow

'Look—there's a hole! He must have squeezed through,' grunted Josh, almost upside down in the compost heap. 'He's gone next door!'

'Can we get through after him?' asked Danny, peering over Josh's shoulder and eyeing the compost heap warily. It was *full* of horrible things, he knew. Worms, beetles, ants, spiders . . . ugh.

'Maybe—if we wriggle . . . ' said Josh.

'Or should we just go round and knock and ask for him back?' Danny said, hopefully. He *really* didn't want to get personal with that heap of horrors.

'What—like a lost ball?' scoffed Josh. 'We've never got one of *those* back before, have we? No . . . I think . . . we can just about . . . '

Josh wriggled and wriggled down through the

warm, moist whiffiness between the back of the
compost heap and the fence. The wood around the
small hole was old and rotten and as Josh pushed
against it more fell away. He squeezed his head and
shoulders through, getting a face full of overgrown
grass, and then crawled right into Miss Potts's
garden. With a few grunts and complaints, Danny
followed, trying not to notice anything scuttling
in the heap. The tickly feeling on his skin was just
grass . . . probably. With a squeak of revulsion he
knocked off a centipede and then hurtled through
the gap after Josh, grazing his left ear.

'Piddle! Piddle!' Josh was calling, softly. No

reply. No patter of little clawed feet. No yap.

The weeds grew up to their waists, filled with invisible chirruping grasshoppers. As Josh and Danny crept through the high grass and nettles they heard one shrill little bark. 'He's gone in her shed!' gasped Danny.

'And *she's* in there!' said Josh, with a gulp. 'She'll be going nuts! We have to go in and rescue him.'

The shed door was open. They tiptoed in. At first it all looked quite normal. There was a rake propped up by the door and a wheelbarrow under some old shelves, full of gardening stuff. An old sheet was hung up on nails at the back.

'It doesn't *smell* like shed,' whispered Danny. 'It smells like . . . like . . . '

'Like school,' said Josh. 'Sort of . . . ' But he couldn't work out exactly why.

'Yes . . . something at school,' agreed Danny, not bothering to whisper now. 'But they're not in here, are they?'

Then there was another bark—and it was *definitely* coming from *inside* the shed. Danny and Josh stared at each other in confusion—and then Danny strode to the back wall, grabbed the old sheet hanging on the nails and pulled it aside. Behind it was a red metal door.

The door was ajar. Pushing it open, Danny saw grey stone steps, leading a short way down to a passage. 'Come on!' Danny went through and Josh followed, staring around him. Wobbly metal panels—corrugated iron, thought Josh—curved up over them in an arch. At the end of the passage

was a well-lit room—as big as their bedroom and Jenny's put together. And in the middle of it, right ahead of them, was a sort of square plastic see-through tent. And in the middle of *that* was Piddle.

The room smelt strange. Very strange. It still reminded him of school—the room where they did science. And there was a hissing noise. Piddle was standing very still, with the fur on his back sticking up. He was scared. 'It's all right, Piddle—we've found you!' said Danny, and pushing the plastic sheeting open, he went into the strange tent. With a swift glance around, noticing some odd machinery and a kind of glass booth, glowing green, off to the left, Josh hurried in after him.

'Come on—let's get out of here! It gives me the heebies,' he said, as Danny gathered the shivering Piddle up into his arms.

Then the hissing got louder—and something cool sprayed across their bare legs.

'What was *that* . . . ?' gasped Danny.

'Don't know! Don't care! Let's go!' replied Josh and they pushed out of the weird tent thing.

Suddenly, Miss Potts's voice rang out. 'Who's

that! Who's in my lab?'

Danny grabbed Josh's arm and they hurtled back along the dark, damp passage.

'HEY! STOP! Come back here!' yelled Miss Potts, and they could hear her thumping across the wooden floor of the weird secret room behind them.

Josh and Danny leapt up the steps, two at a time, and Piddle yelped excitedly over Danny's shoulder, his ears flapping around and his pink tongue hanging out.

'STOP! I know who you ARE!' bellowed Miss Potts.

Danny, Josh, and Piddle almost fell into the garden as Miss Potts's bony hand swatted the sack curtain aside behind them.

'RUN!' gasped Danny. 'RUN!'

Too Many Knees

They hurtled back through the overgrown weeds, shoving Piddle under the fence and scrambling after him as fast as they could go.

Back on their own side, they didn't stop running. Josh and Danny belted straight into the house and upstairs, as if a wild beast was chasing them. It wasn't until they got to the landing that they collapsed in a heap, and started to laugh. Piddle sniffed at their legs, sneezed, and then trotted off into their bedroom.

'Euuurgh!' Danny peered at his legs. They looked kind of—yellow. And they had that weird smell they'd noticed in the secret laboratory. Josh's legs were also covered in the same strange liquid.

'Come on—let's get this stuff off!' said Josh, and they clattered into the bathroom.

'Oi! Don't you two go in there! I'm just about to have my bath!' yelled Jenny, from her bedroom.

'We won't be long!' called back Josh. 'Two minutes!'

They took off their trainers and socks, rolled up their shorts, and stood up in the big bath tub.

'What *is* this stuff?' Danny wrinkled his nose.

'Whatever it is, it's coming off,' said Josh. He grabbed the shower attachment but dropped it.

Then the bath started to grow . . .

Its curved metal rim suddenly shot high, high up beyond their heads and the flat base with its little square of anti-slip bumps suddenly stretched out beneath and around them until it was the size of a basketball court and the bumps were small hills.

AAAAAAA AAaaaaaa . . .

. . . commented Josh.
And Danny agreed.

The plug was now the size of a playground roundabout, hanging off a chain which wouldn't have looked out of place attached to the anchor of a warship.

'AAAAAAAAAAAAAAAAAAAAAAAAAAAAAAAA AAAAAAAAAAH!' added Josh.

Danny went along with that.

At last the growing seemed to stop. They were in a vast white valley of bathtub.

'What's going on?' whimpered Danny. 'What happened to the bath?' His voice sounded a bit funny. Sort of raspy. And also, his eyes felt very odd. He seemed to be able to see round corners at the same time as straight ahead . . .

Behind him came Josh's voice—also a bit raspy. 'Um . . . Danny. Now . . . promise me you'll stay calm.' Josh stared into the shiny mirror-like top of the giant shower attachment which was leaning against the side of the incredibly huge bath. He gulped and blinked some eyes. Yep. His reflection was still the same. He wasn't dreaming it.

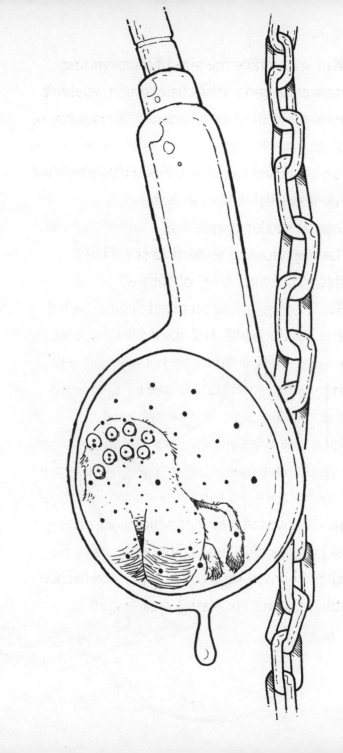

'What *is* that?' Danny found himself moving,
rather smoothly and swiftly, he thought, towards
a huge round well. Above it rested the immense
plug on its gigantic chain. The top of the plug
was also shiny and mirror-like and in it Danny saw
something huge and hairy and standing high on
eight legs. It had eight eyes and a rather surprised
expression. And it MUST BE RIGHT ON TOP
OF HIM!!!!!

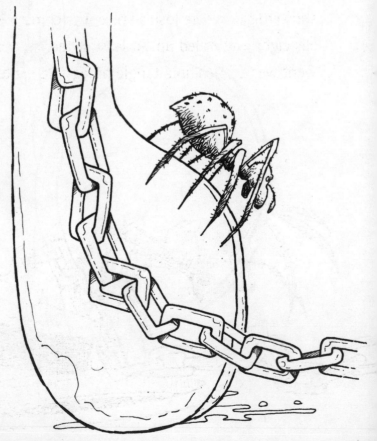

'JO-O-SH! GETITOFF!GETITOFF!GETITOFFME
EEE!!!!, screamed Danny, freaking out. The spider
was freaking out too. It waved its hairy legs wildly
in the giant plug mirror just beyond the giant
plughole.

'I can't get it off you, you dingbat,' shouted Josh.
'It *is* you!'

Danny's mandibles quivered. He looked
around and saw yet another spider over by the
showerhead, where Josh's voice was coming from.
His eight eyes rolled up. At least sixteen knees
went weak. Then, in a tangle of legs, he fainted.

A Hairy Experience

Josh ran across to the collapsed body of his brother. He got hold of Danny's shoulder area—or 'thorax' if he was being correct—using his palps (the little arms on either side of his head) and his two front legs.

'Danny! Wake up!' he shouted in his odd raspy voice. It was probably pointless, though. Danny would most likely just scream and faint again as soon as he saw his brother . . . or his own reflection. Like it or not, believe it or not, they had both just turned into spiders. Josh's brain was doing backflips, trying to take this amazing fact in and work out how it had happened. But he didn't have much time for pondering before he heard a terrible low roaring sound which made the metal under his eight feet vibrate. A shadow fell across him and he looked up to see a horrifying sight.

Jenny.

Screaming.

Raising her gargantuan right hand, in which was grasped a titanic sandal.

Jenny's scream came out incredibly slowly in a weird rumbly voice, as if she had a very sore throat. 'AAAAAAAAAAAAAAAAAH! SPIIIIIIIIIIIIIIIII-DEEE EEEEEEEEEEEEEEEEERRRRRRRRRSSSSSSSSSSSS!'

Her blonde ponytail swung sideways in a huge slow swoop, and her eyes were large and round and shiny. Her vast gaping mouth looked like a terrifying gooey red tunnel.

Even though everything she did was in slow motion, the sandal was now halfway into Bathtub Valley and heading straight for them. They were about to be pulped.

'Dannneee!' screamed Josh, pulling his brother towards the plughole. At last Danny's eyes opened. They started to roll up again as soon as they clapped themselves onto Josh, but Josh cuffed Danny's mandibles with a spare palp and said, 'Cut it out! Don't you dare faint again!

We've got to run!'

Now the sandal was casting a deadly shadow
over them. Josh could smell its rubber sole. He
and Danny ran for it, zipping across to the huge
round black well and then teetering out on its
metal crossbars for just a second, before the sandal
smashed down right next to them. A gust of
rubbery wind knocked them both over and one
second later they were falling down the plughole.

'AAAAAAAAAAAAAARGH!' bellowed
both spiders.

They were plummeting, legs flailing wildly
around them, into a dark, dark hole. Who knew
where it ended? wondered Josh, frantically. It smelt
of soap and old water. Spinning and tumbling,
Josh wondered what it would be like to suffer
eight broken legs. Or maybe have one come off
altogether. Spiders were always losing legs.
That had to hurt!

But the next moment he landed with a thud on something quite soft and springy. The moment after that, his brother landed on top of him.

'Where are we?' Danny whimpered.

'Down the plughole,' said Josh, shoving one of Danny's legs off his face. 'Obviously.'

'But—where—down the plughole?'

Josh looked around. His eyesight was pretty good considering how dark it must be. But of course, most spiders were nocturnal—out and about hunting by night. Danny had scrambled up onto his feet now and was also staring down.

'Oh—oh yuck!' he said. 'You know what this is? What we've landed in?'

'What?' Josh looked at the soggy matter underneath them. It looked like a rather sticky, oozy pile of tangled cables.

'It's Jenny's *hair*! That's what it is!'

Both boys shuddered. 'All those times Mum told her not to let her great clumps of hair go down the plughole after her bath,' said Danny. 'She always said it blocked up the pipes. And now we know she was right. Yeeee-uk!'

43

'Good thing Jenny didn't pay any attention to Mum,' said Josh. 'Her hair gave us a soft landing. She saved our lives.'

Danny shuddered as he looked at Josh. 'Am I really a spider? Just like you? Or am I dreaming this?'

'Yep. You're just like me,' said Josh. 'And I think this is real.'

'Oooow . . . ' wailed Danny. 'I was really hoping this was a dream! How can this be real? How can it?'

'Shhh!' said Josh, looking up into the dark. There was a gurgle above them.

'Ulp,' said Danny.

'She might have saved our lives . . . ' said Josh. There was a splosh.

'But she's trying to kill us again, now!' he screamed. 'She's turned on the TAP!'

A Bit Drained

The water hit them in a big lump, knocking them
off the shelf of hair and on down through the
dark pipe. Plunging down in a whirling, spinning
cascade, Josh felt his legs flapping about in all
directions and prayed that one wouldn't snap off.
Then there was a brief, brilliant flash of light as
they shot out of the end of the downpipe that ran
along the outside of the house, and then all was
dark again as they were carried on down into the
pipework which led to the drain.

Splat! Danny hit a brick and lay draped soggily
over the edge. Splodge! Josh landed on top of him.
They were on a ledge of some kind. Above them
the dark round hole of the pipe dumped still more
water on them, but it was now a light shower.
Then it dwindled to just a few drips. Jenny must

have put the plug in, to run her bath, thought Josh.

Groaning, they gradually untangled their limbs and got up into a sitting position. Below them was a sort of canal through which water slowly flowed. It smelt a bit eggy to Josh. And not in good way. It was dark but a chink of light fed down from the world above them—and he knew that spider sight meant they could see much better than they would have as boys.

'I don't like this,' whimpered Danny.

'You don't say!' muttered Josh.

'Look,' snapped Danny, 'it's bad enough that you're a spider, without being sarcastic too!'

'WE are spiders. Not just me!' grouched back Josh, stepping over a toenail clipping the size of half a bike wheel.

'But—but how? How can this be happening?' gulped Danny. His eight eyes were wide and scared.

'It must have been that yellow stuff,' said Josh. 'It's done something to us.'

'And now we're stuck in a sewer with six more legs than we ever wanted,' groaned Danny. 'And I'm scared to death—of *me!* '

'There are other things you should be scared of, mate!' came an unfamiliar voice. Danny and Josh spun round to look and then all the screaming started again. Towering over them, with glittering black eyes and sharp yellow teeth, was a huge brown hairy monster.

Scratch and Sniff

'Oh, do give it a rest,' said the monster. 'We could hear you screaming all the way down the drainpipe. You should hear yourselves, honestly.'

Josh and Danny stopped screaming and just gulped and gasped a bit instead.

'My name's Scratch,' said the monster, holding out a clawed paw. Danny stared at it and Josh carefully put out a leg to shake.

'And this 'ere is my missus—Sniff.' Another, smaller, monster put her head around the furry shoulder of the first, smiling kindly. 'We live under your shed.'

'Hello, love,' Sniff said. 'Don't look so scared. We won't bite.'

'But . . . but . . . don't you want to eat us?' squeaked Danny.

51

Sniff pulled a face. 'What—spider legs? Stuck in my teeth? I don't think so!'

'We're rats,' went on Scratch. 'We have more refined tastes . . . don't you know? Now, a nice bit of *cake*—oooh yes!'

'Chocolate cake,' sighed Sniff, dreamily. 'With no fluff on.'

Rats! Of course. Now that they were slightly less terrified, Josh and Danny could make out the rodenty shape of Scratch and Sniff.

'And anyway—you're not *proper* spiders, are you?' said Scratch, narrowing his bead-like black eyes.

'Can you tell?' gasped Josh.

'Oh yes. It's the smell,' said Scratch. 'And all the talking. Spiders aren't normally so chatty.'

'You've been got, haven't you, love?' said Sniff. 'By that mad scientist—Petty Potts.'

Danny and Josh scuttled around and exchanged sixteen blinks of surprise.

'Oh you needn't be surprised—we rats know a lot about what humans get up to,' said Scratch with an airy stroke of his whiskers. 'We're your closest cousins, don't you know? Nobody else in the animal world more like humans than rats— we're omnivores and scavengers—just like you!'

'O . . . K,' said Josh. 'But what can you tell us about Petty Potts? Exactly *what* has she done to us?'

'It's her SWITCH spray,' said Scratch. 'She's been working on it for years in that secret lab of hers. We pop in from time to time for the sandwiches (she never finishes a cheese and

pickle!). Anyway, she finally made a breakthrough
a few weeks ago—and started to SWITCH things!'

'*Switch* things?' said Danny.

'S-W-I-T-C-H,' said Scratch. 'It stands for . . .
now . . . let me think . . . '

'Serum Which Instigates Total Cellular Hijack!'
said Sniff, suddenly sounding like a chemistry
professor.

'Um . . . what?' said Danny.

'It's a serum—that's what she calls it,' went on
Sniff. 'It forces all your body cells to be different
kinds of cells . . . like each cell has been hijacked
by another cell, you see? So—Serum Which
Instigates Total Cellular Hijack! We've only
heard her say it about a hundred and fifty times!
She spent *ages* trying to come up with a smart
sounding name—she was going to call it Serum To
Initiate Process Of Morphing . . . but STIPOM just
doesn't roll off the tongue so well.'

'How do you *know* all these words?' gasped
Danny. 'I mean . . . you're *rats*!'

'Danny!' Josh poked his brother with one hairy
leg. 'Rats are very intelligent!'

54

'Well, we watch a lot of TV,' said Sniff.

'Hear a lot of Radio Four, too,' said Scratch.

'Anyway, at first she was just doing little things with this SWITCH spray,' went on Sniff. 'Insects. A bee into an ant—a beetle into a spider.'

'Not an insect—an arachnid,' pointed out Josh.

'Is he always like this?' Sniff asked Danny.

'Yes,' Danny sighed. 'He's a freaky little bug boffin.'

'So,' went on Sniff, 'just tiny creatures at first, and we thought that was all there was to it. But only this week she was saying she wanted to try the SWITCH spray on bigger things. Reptiles, perhaps—maybe even mammals! We kept *well* out of her way when we heard that!'

'Good job she talks out loud to herself,' added Scratch. 'Or we might never have known. She had her eye on us I can tell you! In fact she was just setting a rat trap for *us* when your little dog came in and weed on her floor.'

'So she was trying to SWITCH Piddle into a bug? Horrible woman!' said Danny.

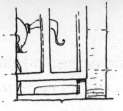

'Yes—but she got you instead,' said Scratch.
'We saw it all from under the sink in her lab. That's
why we came to find you. We heard you up in
your bathroom, then heard your big sister shrieking
about two spiders in the bath—and put two and
two together. It doesn't take long for the spray
to work. Sometimes it goes off in seconds! We
worked out where you would've ended up—down
the plughole!' Scratch chuckled and shook his
head. 'And as your closest cousins, well, it was
only right to try and help.'

'Well . . . er . . . thanks,' said Josh, resisting the
urge to correct Scratch. Apes were *actually* their
closest cousins, but it seemed impolite to say so.
'But what do we do now?'

'Well, get out of here for a start,' said Scratch.
'It's not safe. Get on our backs and we'll swim you
out of here.' Doubtfully, the brothers looked at the
rats' backs as Scratch and Sniff shimmied down
low to let the spiders climb on board.

'Go on, love,' Sniff encouraged Josh. 'Just hang
on to my fur and you won't fall off.'

Josh went for it. He just ran up Sniff's back and
found it surprisingly easy. There were clever little
hooks on the bottom of each of his feet which
anchored him tightly onto her fur. Danny ran up
onto Scratch a moment later and then, with a
whoosh of eggy air, Scratch leapt into the slow-
moving stream and began to swim along the sewer.

The dark water surged up and Danny ran up onto Scratch's head, alarmed. It was quite flat on top, between his ears, and easy to hang on to. Behind swam Sniff, her nose held daintily above the water and Josh also anchored between her ears.

'Oh no—we're not going down to the bit where the poos come out, are we?' fretted Danny. But a moment later they came out into daylight. They were swimming through the small stream in the little overgrown gully which ran along between the back gardens in their road and the next road along. 'Phew! No poo!' sighed Danny.

'I should think *not*,' sniffed Sniff. 'We do have our standards, you know!'

'Thank you,' said Josh, running down Sniff's soaked back and onto a large stone at the edge of the stream. 'Now can you tell us how we get back to being humans?'

Scratch and Sniff, shaking the water out of their fur on a tiny beach of pebbles below them, exchanged worried glances as Danny joined Josh on the rock.

'You don't—you don't mean to tell us . . . that we're like this for good?' gasped Josh.

'Well . . . er . . . no,' said Scratch. 'We don't know that for sure . . . and in fact I know that one of the bees turned back into a bee after just a few hours as an ant . . .'

'*One* of them? What happened to the other ones that Petty Potts got with her SWITCH spray?' demanded Josh.

'Well—they *might* have changed back . . . if there had been time,' said Scratch, looking rather awkward. 'Only . . . well . . . most of them got . . .'

'Got? Got what?' squawked Danny, standing up high on his legs like a very unattractive ballerina.

'Eaten,' sighed Sniff. 'Most things get eaten.
I mean . . . a lot of things get eaten *anyway*,
but when you're an ant or a bee or a beetle or
something, you get to know how to look out
for yourself. If you're suddenly SWITCHed into
something else you get . . . well . . . confused.
And if you're confused you're . . . well . . . lunch!'

'Josh,' said Danny, edging towards his brother,
even though he was still terrified of his legs,
'I don't know about you—but I'm confused. I'm
very confused.'

'Me too,' gulped Josh and that's when the icky
sticky pink thing suddenly ickily stickily stuck to
his shoulder—and he was yanked high into the air.

Lunch

The worst thing about being a freaky little bug boffin was knowing *too* much.

And the worst thing about being a spider was being able to think so much faster than a human. Josh had read, in his many wildlife books, that everything moves so much faster in the world of spiders and insects, that they must think quickly to survive. And now he knew it was true, as he flew through the air, stuck to the pink thing. He had time to work out quite a few things.

He worked out, first of all, that he was stuck to the tongue of a toad.

Then he worked out that he was probably not going to un-stick himself.

Then he worked out that he was probably going to be eaten . . . ALIVE!

He knew that toads eat their prey alive. They don't mind *at all* if their lunch kicks and complains as it goes down. For the first time ever in his life, Josh wished he hadn't read so many wildlife books.

As he flew helplessly towards the toad's gaping mouth, Josh twisted round, got hold of some of the long, long tongue, drove his fangs into it and squirted some venom in. The tongue didn't let go. There was no hope. He was toad take-away.

CRUNCH.

SPLAT.

SQUISH.

That's the end of me, then, thought Josh. *Funny. Only felt a little bump!* He opened one eye. Then six or seven more. The sticky tongue was still attached to his shoulder (or thorax if he was being correct) but the other end was no longer attached to a toad. It lay flattened under a giant black boot.

Someone had stamped on the toad! STAMPED on it!

Behind him Josh could hear anguished cries from Danny and Scratch and Sniff. They must think he was done for. Josh stood up, finding all his legs were shaking with fright, and then ran away before whoever it was could stamp on him too. The tongue followed him. Eeeeuuugh! It came away from the edge of the boot and then snaked along behind him like a weird scarf, skipping and bouncing over the rocks and fallen trees, which had once been just twigs and pebbles when he was a boy.

As he reached Danny and their rat friends Josh yelled—for the first time ever—'GETTITOFF—GETTITOFF—GETTITOFFMEEEEEEEE!'

Scratch leant over and tugged the half a tongue with his teeth. It squelched and popped as it finally came off.

'We thought you was a goner, son!' said Scratch, after spitting out the tongue and hustling them all beneath an old log. 'We thought you was lunch! Nobody's ever got away from Gripper. Not ever! If he hadn't just got stamped on you'd be down his throat by now.'

Poor Josh gulped and Danny went to put a comforting arm . . . er . . . leg . . . around him . . . but just couldn't make that work somehow. (*Who ever got comfort from a spider's leg?* he wondered.) 'We've *got* to find a way to get back to being humans again,' he said. 'Or we'll never make it to teatime.'

'Well, I hate to say it,' said Sniff. 'But Petty Potts is most likely the only one who can help you.'

'But how will she know it's us? She might just stamp on us like someone just stamped on that toad,' squeaked Danny. He looked around, anxiously, but the owner of the boot, who had been screened from view by the leaves of a large bush, seemed to have gone.

'No, she wouldn't stamp on you. She never wastes insects,' said Scratch.

'Arachnids,' corrected Josh and everyone gave him a *look*.

'And didn't you see? It *was* Petty Potts who just stamped on Gripper,' added Scratch. 'She was probably after him for another one of her experiments. He peered out from under the log . . . She's made a gap in her back fence so she can get down here and kidnap innocent creatures for her lab! Can't see her now though. She must have gone back with Gripper's gooey bits. I think we should take you back there, too. Maybe she'll help you. Maybe you can find a way to show her who you are.'

'Well, at least let's check for any more toads, before we go,' said Josh, with a shiver.

He edged out from under the log, looked all around—and then ran up a tree. Yes! He ran

right up it so fast he shocked himself. 'Look at me!
Danny! Look at me! I'm up the tree!' he yelled,
excitedly, quite forgetting to be afraid.

Danny lost no time in catching up. He was
the sporty one, after all, and he wasn't going to
be beaten to the top by Josh. 'Woo-hoo!' he called,
overtaking Josh. 'I'm a superhero! I can walk
up walls!!!'

'Steady now,' called up Scratch from the lower
part of the trunk, where he was scrabbling a little

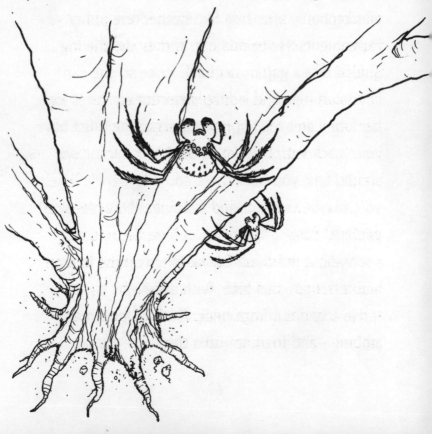

way up. 'Lots of things up there looking for lunch! Best come down.'

But Josh and Danny had now run along to the tip of a high branch and were staring, amazed, at the view. From here they could see across their garden and into the gardens on either side—and everything lay below them like half the country, seen from an aeroplane. So incredibly colourful and interesting and BIG! Butterflies flapped past them like giant kites, bees and flies zoomed in all directions, sounding like helicopters and never bumping into each other, as if they were being guided by air traffic control.

A slurping noise above them turned out to be a chubby green caterpillar munching through a leaf. It burped. It winked a big black eye at them. It went 'Pardon.'

'Oooh—lovely! Leggy snackage! I was feeling peckish,' came a voice just behind them. Danny spun about in horror. Above them on the branch was a humungous bird. A blackbird, he thought. It had a bright orange beak. And the beak was jabbing right down towards them.

'AAAAAAAAAARGH!'

Danny ran up the branch and then found
himself sliding off the edge. For one horrible
second he tipped sideways into thin air, ready to
plummet down—and then he realized he was still
running. He ran right round under the branch, Josh
hot on his many heels. All of a sudden the world
was upside down. Their incredible little hooky feet
were keeping them attached to the craggy bark of
the tree. They were defying gravity!

'Like Spiderman!' marvelled Josh, under his
breath.

'Has it gone?' whispered Danny.

For a few seconds they hung there, petrified.
Then there was a terrifyingly loud whistle and a
huge black feathered head swung round the branch
and gaped its beak at them.

'Aah—nearly lost you,' it said. 'Brace yourself.
Got the munchies.'

'Noooooooo!' shouted both Josh and Danny,
while below they could hear Scratch and Sniff
desperately shouting at the bird to get away.

'Now look!' said the bird, tilting its head on
one side and regarding them patiently. 'Stop faffin'
about. I need a snack and you're it. That's the
pecking order. Get over it.'

'Drop!' yelled Josh. 'Just let go!'

Danny didn't need telling. He'd rather splatter
on the ground than get eaten alive. He let go and
found himself once again wheeling around in
freefall.

Ooh. *That* was an unexpectedly soft landing.

As Danny lay, dazed, he realized he was on
some kind of material. A short distance away Josh
was also flopped onto the material, feverishly

73

counting his legs. Danny looked at the criss-cross of green and brown wool threads. From its round shape and a few grey cables of hair on it, he guessed it was a hat. And now it was tipping up.

Shrieking, Josh and Danny ran up the material, grabbing hold after hold with their hooky feet, but whoever was holding the hat determinedly shook it until they fell again, this time with a plop, into a large see-through container. Inside it Josh ran round and round, shooting something weird out of his bottom.

'Eeeuw!' said Danny. 'Spiderman never did it like *that*!'

Josh was making an emergency web— shooting silk out of the spinner on his abdomen to create a network of strong rope, which he was sticking all over the see-through plastic at very high speed as he ran round. They would be able to use it to climb up.

But Danny could see it was hopeless. Above them a lid crashed down shut. And now the super-sized face of none other than Petty Potts loomed slowly into view, peering in at them. Josh could see mammoth bristly hairs up inside her cavernous pink nostrils.

He slumped down into his useless emergency web and sighed: 'I really didn't ever want to see that.'

A Bit of Gas

'OOOOOOOOOOOOOOOH
DDDEEEEEEEEEEEEEEEAR!' roared Petty Potts,
in a slow deep voice.

'TIIIIIIIIIIIIIIME TOOOOOO
GEEET YOUUUUUUUUU
SSSSSSSSSOOOOOOOOOORRRRRRRTED
OOOOOOOOOUUUUUUUUT.'

Josh felt quite sea-sick as their plastic tub
carriage swung along in the old lady's hands.
He clung on tightly to the stout see-through silk
cables which he had unexpectedly produced. He
was rather proud of his web, in fact. Even if it *had*
come out of his backside.

Danny was hanging on too, his furry face
looking rather green. 'Now what?' he whimpered.

Josh thought hard. He didn't think Petty Potts

would hurt them—deliberately—but maybe she would want to experiment on them. After all, it sounded as if she knew who they were and she must be pretty excited. She had succeeded in turning two mammals into spiders!

At last they reached the huge dark cave of her laboratory behind the shed. She set their tub down on a gigantic table, and peeled off the lid. She spoke at them but it was too roary and loud and slow to make any sense. Her big warm gusts of breath smelt like cheese.

A short while later there were two thuds and

two dark bundles, wrapped in white material, bounced down between them. They smelt fantastic. Danny suddenly realized how incredibly hungry he was. These were flasks of hot meaty soup! He was sure of it. He could smell it. He scuttled across to one of them and quickly ripped off the wrapping. The flask had six legs, two wings and an anxious expression, but Danny didn't stop to think about this. Yum! The soup was great!

It was only when he'd gulped it all down that he noticed the look on Josh's face. His brother's mandibles were stuck up straight like shocked fingers and one of his eyes twitched. 'Nice lunch?' he whispered.

'Ah . . . yes,' admitted Danny. 'Er . . . bluebottle soup. Not Heinz, but not bad.' He shuddered and felt a little queasy.

'ARGH!' said Josh and Danny agreed with him. The tub was tipping up and they were sliding out onto the table top. The surface was cold stone of some kind—quite smooth. Now a glass bowl was slammed, upside down, over them and through a round gap in the top a yellowish fog was hissing and blooming down.

'She's killing us! We're done for!' whimpered Danny. But Josh thought he was wrong. It would be much easier to kill them with a shoe than with gas. A few seconds later, though, he wasn't so sure. His head felt funny and his legs gave way and his ears were all muffled and . . . and . . . and . . .

'Can't say I ever thought you two would be

welcome in my lab—but today has changed my mind and no mistake,' said Petty Potts. She had stopped roaring and her mammoth face was now back to its usual size, Danny realized. He sat up, his legs—just the two of them now—dangling off the edge of the table.

'You—ba—ca—wa—you—ca—wa—ba—you!' he spluttered.

'Yes, I know what you mean,' she said, beaming, her brown eyes lively behind their rather smeary glasses. Now Josh sat up, making similar noises.

'I know exactly what you want to say. Why on earth would I change you both into spiders, yes? Well—I didn't—not deliberately. I *was* having a crack at changing your little wee-soaked dog into a spider, I admit—but then you two blundered in and got the SWITCH spray up your legs instead. You know, I *did* try to stop you running off into danger. You're lucky to be alive. If I hadn't found you in time, stamped on that toad, frightened those rats off and then whipped you away from that blackbird, you'd be floating in some creature's digestive juices by now.'

'Well, thanks!' muttered Josh.

'How *did* you find us?' asked Danny. 'We were tiny!'

'Aah!' Petty Potts held up a small device which looked a bit like a mini torch. A blue light flashed on the end of it and it gave off a crackly noise. 'This is a SWITCHee Detector. It only works within about ten feet of a SWITCHed creature, but it's a help when they wander off. It gets brighter and louder, the closer I get.'

'You do realize we could be dead by now—

thanks to you?' said Danny, glaring at her. 'Or if your gadget thingy hadn't worked we'd be spiders for life!'

'No, you wouldn't. The SWITCH spray doesn't last.' Petty Potts sighed and shook her head. 'I haven't quite perfected it. But I also have an antidote for emergencies, which I just used on you. Thought you might like a little snack first, though—so dropped in a couple of flies, already prepared by another spider behind my fridge. I guess it was Danny who scoffed one, was it?' Danny nodded, looking a little green. 'So—tell me! What does it taste like?' She perched on a stool and stared at him. Danny stared back at her, horrified.

'And how was it? To be a spider? It must have been so exciting!' She was nodding and smiling at both of them now. There was a notebook and pen in her hand. 'SPIDER-SWITCH is my latest spray. I wasn't sure it would work, as it's an arachnid serum, not an insect one. And of course, I've never tried any of my SWITCH sprays on mammals until today. So—what does it feel like?'

Danny snapped. He jumped off the table. 'What do you think it feels like, you mad granny?' he squawked. 'Terrifying, that's what! We've been nearly flattened, drowned, eaten and pecked to death!'

Petty Potts sighed again and nodded some more. 'I can see it's been a bit upsetting for you. Why don't you come to tea tomorrow and tell me all about it then?'

'You must be joking!' said Danny. 'We will NEVER, EVER set foot on this side of the fence again. EVER. And don't you ever come over our side! If you want to find out what it feels like to be changed into a spider—SWITCH yourself!'

They jumped off the table and ran back home barefoot, scraping through the gap in the fence at high speed and never looking back.

Back in her lab, Petty Potts smiled to herself. She picked up a little red velvet box from a high shelf, and lifted the lid, revealing six shiny glass cubes, each with a tiny hologram of an insect or bug inside it, and a series of strange symbols running along beneath it. Danny would have recognized

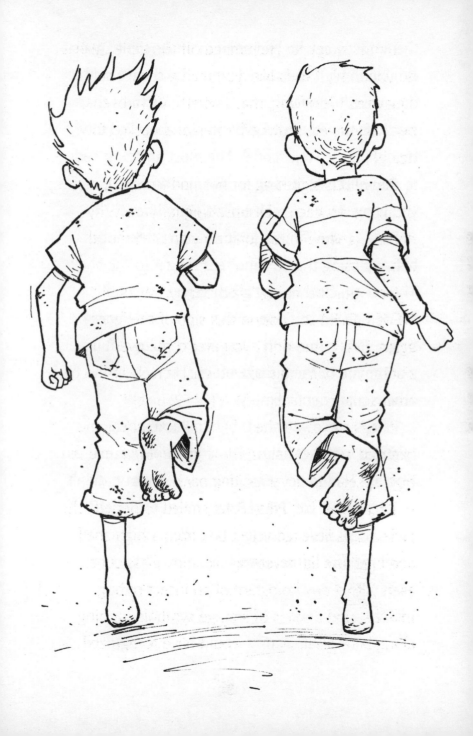

them. Last week he had been to an Ancient Egypt exhibition with the school, and would have said they were 'hieroglyphics'—the mini pictures that made up the Ancient Egyptian alphabet. To Petty, though, these were 'code'. The most amazing code to the most astonishing formula in the world, if you know how to crack it. And Petty knew.

Petty ran her fingers lovingly across the cubes before closing the box and returning it to the shelf. Then she picked up the green velvet box beside it. She opened this one with a sigh. Inside was a single glass cube, with a tiny lizard hologram inside it and more of the hieroglyphics. There were five other square dents. Empty.

Petty's smile vanished. She thwacked her forehead with her palm. 'Oh, you stupid, stupid old woman! Had to get your memory burnt out, didn't you?! What if you NEVER find them again, eh? Then you'll never get the *next* code—and you'll never get any further than bugs!'

Hair Today

'Danny! I can't believe you're not eating your cake!' said Mum, staring at Danny's uneaten tea in astonishment.

Danny gave her a wobbly smile. 'Um—it's just that I'm still full since . . . since . . . lunch.' When he remembered what he'd last eaten his smile went even more wobbly.

'He ate the insides of a bluebottle earlier,' said Josh, through a mouthful of his chocolate cake. Danny flinched. 'It wasn't quite dead, either.'

'Ooh—you two are so revolting and creepy,' shuddered Jenny, her hair still wrapped up in a towel. She'd only got out of the bath five minutes ago; she could set a world record for staying in a bath, reading magazines. 'Stop talking about disgusting things or I'll kill you both!'

'Not again,' moaned Danny. 'You've already tried twice today.'

He got up and went into the garden with his cake. He went to the shed, knelt down and then put the plate down next to it. Josh followed him. 'What are you doing?' he asked.

'Seeing if Scratch and Sniff are in,' said Danny. 'They told us they live under our shed, remember?'

'Oh yeah,' said Josh and sat down next to Danny. 'We never did thank them for saving our lives.'

Behind him there were squeaks—and then
the familiar snouts of Scratch and Sniff emerged,
twitching at the lovely scent in the air.

'This is to say thanks,' said Danny, tipping the
cake off the plate. 'You probably can't really work
out what I'm saying—but thanks anyway. For
looking after me and Josh.' Sniff clasped her little
paws together and rolled her eyes with delight. 'No
fluff on it,' said Danny.

'See you around,' said Josh as their friends bit
into the cake and dragged the whole thing back
under the shed with little grunts of effort and
delight.

'Maybe we won't,' said Danny. 'I think we
should probably just forget the whole thing!
Nothing like that will ever happen again. We've
blocked up the fence so Piddle can't get through.
And we never go next door—ever again.'

'Too right,' said Josh. 'I love wildlife—but I don't
want to *be* it.'

Danny and Josh ran inside. Jenny was holding
her hairdryer, the lead stretched round to the plug
just outside the downstairs toilet where she liked

to do her hair and make-up. She stalked out and ripped the plug out of the socket, huffing and glaring at Mum through a curtain of wet hair.

'How many times do I have to tell you, Jenny?' snapped Mum. 'STOP drying your hair over the sink.'

'NO!' shouted Danny. 'Let her! Let her dry her hair over the sink! It saves lives!'

Jenny and Mum stared at him—and at Josh who was nodding vigorously in agreement.

'I tell you, Mum,' said Jenny, pointing at them with the hairdryer. 'They're another species these two. Another species!'

DIARY ENTRY *562.4

SUBJECT: JOSH AND DANNY PHILLIPS

Have made a breakthrough! Those ghastly eight year olds from next door got sprayed by mistake! Managed to rescue them, though, before they got eaten. Asked what being a spider was like but they were hysterical. Will try again tomorrow.

Good news! They can't get away from me. They live only yards away. And as they are children, nobody will ever believe what happened, so my secret is safe. And anyway, I think it's high time I had some assistants on the SWITCH PROJECT. I've been working alone for far too long.

REMEMBER

$$\frac{4 \times \Pi^2}{OS-7*} \quad \frac{P_2}{0.8} \times \frac{V_6^2\%/9}{2\,\Pi_5\frac{0}{T}} = \frac{4.198}{4.197} \frac{}{(543)}$$

S.W.I.T.C.H

If ONLY I could REMEMBER what happened to the rest of my research! I know I put the code for SWITCHing creatures to reptiles in the crystal cubes, as I did for the bugs and insects formula . . . and I know I hid the cubes somewhere SAFE. Too safe. Safe from even me!!! I just can't remember. Victor Crouch has a lot to answer for. I will get my revenge on him, for burning out chunks of my memory and trying to steal my life's work. If I ever see him again I will SWITCH him into a cockroach and stamp on him.

But with two young brains to help me, I might be able to find the lost Reptile SWITCH cubes and finally rediscover all my brilliant work.

I will recruit Josh and Danny tomorrow. I am sure I can persuade them to help me with my research—and also to continue the hunt for the missing cubes.

Yes, I am sure I will find a way to convince them.

After all . . . what boy wouldn't want to transform into a giant python or a crocodile one day . . . ?

$$\frac{60}{\frac{OUP}{\pi}} \rightarrow \cancel{\not{\rho}} \rightarrow \frac{1}{2}St^2$$

ARACHNID

GLOSSARY

Abdomen—The main part of a spider's body.

Antidote—A medicine that can reverse the effects of a poison.

Arachnid—Another name for a spider. Arachnids are joint-legged (have more than one joint on each leg) and are invertebrates (animals without spines).

Cellular—Something made from a group of living cells.

Hieroglyphics—Ancient Egyptian pictures and symbols that represent words.

Hijack—To take control of something by force.

Hologram—A picture made up of laser beams which appear three dimensional (3D).

Insects—Animals with six legs and three body parts; the head, thorax and abdomen.

Mammals—Animals that give birth to live young and feed them with their own milk. Humans and rats are mammals.

Mandibles—Lie either side of a spider's mouth and are used for clutching food.

GLOSSARY

Morphing—The process by which an object changes into something else. For example, Danny and Josh morph from boys into spiders.

Nocturnal—Animals that hunt at night and rest during the day.

Omnivore—An animal which can eat plants or other animals. Humans are omnivores.

Palps—Feelers which spiders use to search for food.

Prey—An animal that is hunted by another animal for food.

Reptiles—Cold-blooded animals. Lizards and snakes are reptiles.

Scavengers—Animals that gather things discarded by others or that eat the remains of prey left by another animal.

Thorax—The section of a spider's body between the head and abdomen.

Venom—Poison that can be squirted from the fangs of an animal to kill or stun its prey. Some spiders are venomous.

PLACES TO VISIT

Want to brush up on your bug knowledge?
Here's a list of places with special areas
dedicated to creepy-crawlies.

Liverpool Museum

http://www.liverpoolmuseums.org.uk/wml/
naturalworld/bughouse/

Marwell Wildlife Park

http://www.marwell.org.uk/

Natural History Museum

http://www.nhm.ac.uk/

Remember, you don't need
to go far to find your favourite
bugs. Why not venture out
into your garden or the
park and see how many
different creatures
you can spot.

WEBSITES

Find out more about nature and wildlife
using the websites below.

http://www.bbc.co.uk/cbbc/wild/

http://www.nhm.ac.uk/kids-only/

http://kids.nationalgeographic.com/

http://www.switch-books.co.uk/

Another exciting adventure awaits . . .

Horror at the Hedge

'Buzz off, you revolting little pest!' Jenny
thwacked Danny on the head with her rolled-up
magazine.

Josh tried not to giggle. His sister had been
reading peacefully for five minutes, unaware
that Danny was crouched on the back of the
sofa behind her, rubbing the backs of his hands
together, poking out his tongue and rolling his
eyes madly. A half eaten biscuit in her hand,
Jenny hadn't even noticed Josh standing in the
doorway, taking pictures with his little digital
camera.

It was only when Danny started buzzing that
things turned ugly.

'Go and play outside, you creepy little
horrors!' yelled Jenny, who was fourteen, so

thought she could boss them around. She whacked Danny again and he fell off the sofa and rolled across the sitting room floor, laughing and buzzing.

Josh tucked his camera into his pocket and strolled out towards the front garden with his twin brother. 'Of course, if you really wanted to be a fly, you should have spat stomach acid on her Jammy Dodger, walked all over it until it was mush and then eaten it.'

Danny biffed the back of Josh's neat fair head as they went down the hallway. 'And Mum says I'm the disgusting one!'

'It's just nature,' shrugged Josh, biffing Danny back on his spiky fair head. 'Flies are amazing—I can show you one under my microscope if you like.'

'Yuck! I don't like!' shuddered Danny. It was one thing pretending to be an insect to annoy Jenny, but he hated the real thing.

'You ate one quite happily a couple of weeks ago,' Josh reminded him.

Danny stopped dead on the front doorstep. 'I thought we agreed never to talk about that again!'

'Well, yeah, but—'

'NEVER!' said Danny.

Outside, Mum was by the front hedge, talking to Mrs Sharpe from down the road. The garden looked fantastic—carefully trimmed and mown and full of flowers, bushes, and little trees, all overflowing with colourful blossom. The hedge, though, was her real pride and joy. For years she had trimmed and trained it into three little bird shapes along the top. It was a special skill called 'topiary', she had explained to Josh and Danny. She called them her 'hedge birds'.

'Come to help with the weeding, boys?' she asked, when she saw them. Mum had gone in for the Best Garden competition in their village. Last year she'd come third, and this year she was determined to win. Piddle, their terrier dog, had been banned from going anywhere near the front garden. He was shut in the back garden today, out of harm's way. 'Can't see any weeds!' said Josh.

'There are some there,' said Mrs Sharpe, pointing at the rose bed. 'And over by the marigolds. Quite a few really. Of course, my garden is completely weed free now—with only one day to go before judging, I couldn't possibly allow anything wild to start messing it up.' She smiled smugly at them all. 'Have to make sure I keep the cup again this year, don't I, Tarquin?'

A thin, pale boy of about Josh and Danny's age slithered around from behind his mother, and gave their garden a look of great disdain. 'I think your trophy is quite safe, Mother,' he said, in a high-pitched voice.

'Well,' said Mum, twisting a dead rose bloom off its stalk with some force. 'How nice to have such a

supportive son, Mrs Sharpe.'

'He is a darling,' sighed Mrs Sharpe. 'And did I tell you that he scored top in his whole school for maths this week? He's Mummy's little genius!' She patted Tarquin's neatly parted dark hair. 'Of course, not every child can be a genius, can they?' She smiled pityingly at Josh and Danny. 'But that doesn't matter, does it?'

Danny made 'being sick' noises and Tarquin pulled ugly faces at them.

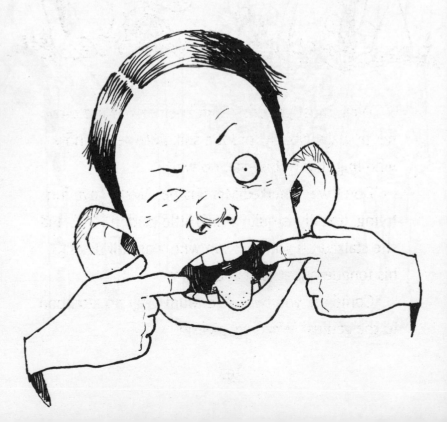

'Well, must get on!' Mum knelt down and drove her trowel viciously into the soil. 'We never know who might win this year, do we?'

'Don't we?' smirked Mrs Sharpe. 'Well, have fun trying. It really is quite a nice little garden . . . ' And she stalked off with her son who was still poking his tongue out at Josh and Danny.

'Come on, you two,' said Mum. 'Pay no attention to the genius! Weeding, please!'

Josh and Danny worked their way along the wall, pulling out very tiny weeds and throwing them into Mum's wheelbarrow. 'Weee-aaargh!' shrieked Danny, wildly flapping his hand. A small spider dropped off it and scuttled away.

'You know, I'm surprised you haven't got over your fear of spiders,' said Josh, quietly. 'Considering you've *been* a spider.'

'*DON'T* remind me!' Danny looked around warily for more eight-legged foes. 'I'm trying to forget it ever happened.'

'What—that we got hit by Miss Potts's SWITCH spray? And we got changed into spiders, fell down the bathplug, got rescued by rats, nearly eaten by a toad and a blackbird and then got made human again—all before tea?' Josh grinned as Danny narrowed his eyes at him.

'I don't know how you can be so calm about it!' grunted Danny, brutally pulling up a dandelion.

'I'm not!' said Josh. 'It gives me the shivers just to think about Petty Potts, hidden away in her secret lab behind the shed, turning all kinds of poor creatures into bugs just for fun. But it was kind of exciting, too—wasn't it? And she did turn us back again.'

'Exciting? It was terrifying! I was a spider! A spider! I was scared of my own legs!'

Josh chucked another handful of weeds into the wheelbarrow. 'Well, don't worry. It's all in the past now. We haven't even seen Petty Potts since. And we're never going next door again!'

'Ah!' said their mum, to someone at the gate. 'Good timing! I'm just about to go to the garden centre now. Is it still OK for the boys to come round to your house?'

Danny and Josh looked up from their weeding. Their mouths fell open in horror.

Standing by the hedge was their next-door neighbour—Petty Potts.

FUN AND GAMES

There are more games for you to play and download free on the S.W.I.T.C.H. website.

www.switch-books.co.uk

Word search

Search for the hidden words listed below:

DANNY   SPRAY

JOSH   HOLOGRAM

PIDDLE   TOP SECRET

PETTY POTTS   SPIDERS

SCRATCH   HAIRY

SNIFF   DRAIN

SWITCH   JENNY

D	J	E	N	N	Y	R	I	A	H
W	A	S	R	E	D	I	P	S	T
I	Y	N	D	R	A	I	N	W	O
F	F	I	N	S	B	X	J	I	P
P	E	T	T	Y	P	O	T	T	S
S	W	U	J	O	S	H	F	C	E
H	L	T	S	P	R	A	Y	H	C
P	S	C	R	A	T	C	H	B	R
E	L	D	D	I	P	K	A	T	E
M	A	R	G	O	L	O	H	K	T

Spot the difference

These pictures *look* the same, but can you spot ten differences?

True or false?

1) A fear of spiders is called arachnophobia.

2) There are around 38,000 species of spider in the world.

3) All spiders are poisonous.

4) Spider webs can help stop wounds from bleeding.

5) Every species of spider can make a web.

6) Male spiders are bigger than female spiders.

7) Some species of spider live in the Arctic.

8) Some spiders are so light they can walk on water.

9) Spiders belong to the insect family.

10) Spiders have 72 knees.

Answers on page 122

Missing piece

Can you work out which piece of the puzzle is missing?

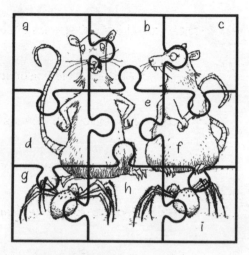

Answer on page 122

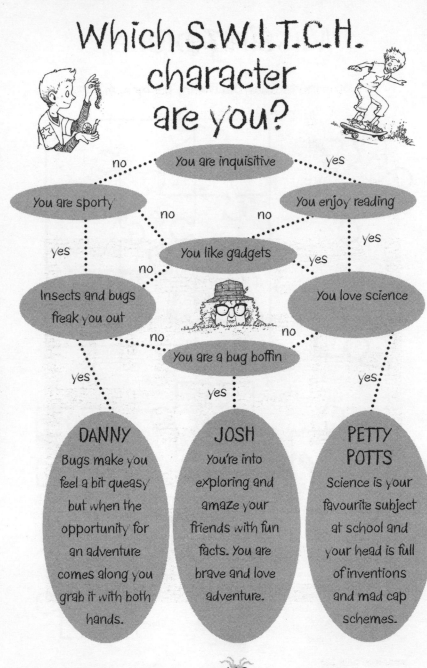

Which S.W.I.T.C.H. character are you?

You are inquisitive — no / yes

You are sporty

You enjoy reading — yes

no — no

You like gadgets

yes

yes

no

Insects and bugs freak you out

You love science

no — no

You are a bug boffin

yes

yes

yes

DANNY
Bugs make you feel a bit queasy but when the opportunity for an adventure comes along you grab it with both hands.

JOSH
You're into exploring and amaze your friends with fun facts. You are brave and love adventure.

PETTY POTTS
Science is your favourite subject at school and your head is full of inventions and mad cap schemes.

Maze

Can you help Josh and Danny get through the maze to rescue Piddle?

Answer on page 123

Board game

You have been turned into a spider and have to get across the garden to Petty Potts's laboratory. The player who gets there first is the winner.

For this game you will need one die, a tiddlywink (or something of a similar size) for each player and two or more players.

START The Garden 1	Scratch and Sniff carry you on their backs. Move ahead 2 squares. 2	 3
  6	 5	 4
You've been spotted by a toad! Scuttle back 2 squares. 7	 8	It's Petty Potts's big boot! Quick, run forward one square. 9
  12	This bird looks peckish. You had better hide. Miss a go. 11	 10
Yum! You are distracted by a tasty fly soup snack. Miss a go. 13	 14	**FINISH** Congratulations! You have made it to Petty Potts's laboratory. 15

Are you a bug boffin?

Question 1)
WHAT ARE PALPS?
A) Another name for spiders' legs
B) Feelers which a spider uses when looking for food
C) The body of a spider

Question 2)
HOW MANY LEGS DOES A SPIDER HAVE?
A) 8
B) 2
C) 9

Question 3)
WHAT DOES S.W.I.T.C.H. STAND FOR?
A) Spray Which Instigates Terrible Cellular Hijack
B) Some Wicked Invention To Change Humans
C) Serum Which Instigates Total Cellular Hijack

Question 4)
SCRATCH AND SNIFF ARE OMNIVORES WHICH MEANS THEY ARE:
A) Rats
B) Animals that can eat plants or animals
C) Animals that can be in two places at once

Question 5)
WHAT IS AN ARACHNID?
A) A spider
B) One of Petty Potts's gadgets
C) A type of bird

Question 6)
WHICH TWO PREDATORS DO JOSH AND DANNY COME ACROSS IN THE GARDEN AFTER THEY'VE BEEN TURNED INTO SPIDERS?
A) Fox and frog
B) Toad and bird
C) Cat and dog

Question 7)
WHAT IS JOSH AND DANNY'S DOG CALLED?
A) Piddle
B) Riddle
C) Widdle

Question 8)
WHY IS PETTY POTTS SO FORGETFUL?
A) She tripped and banged her head in her laboratory
B) Victor Crouch wiped parts of her memory
C) She experimented on herself and wiped parts of her own memory

Answers on page 123

Answers

Word search (page 114)

D	J	E	N	N	Y	R	I	A	H
W	A	S	R	E	D	I	P	S	T
I	Y	N	D	R	A	I	N	W	O
F	F	I	N	S	B	X	J	I	P
P	E	T	T	Y	P	O	T	T	S
S	W	U	J	O	S	H	F	C	E
H	L	T	S	P	R	A	Y	H	C
P	S	C	R	A	T	C	H	B	R
E	L	D	D	I	P	K	A	T	E
M	A	R	G	O	L	O	H	K	T

Spot the difference (page 115)

True or False
(page 116)

1) True
2) True
3) False
4) True
5) False
6) False
7) True
8) True
9) False
10) False

Missing piece
(page 117)

Answers

Maze (page 119)

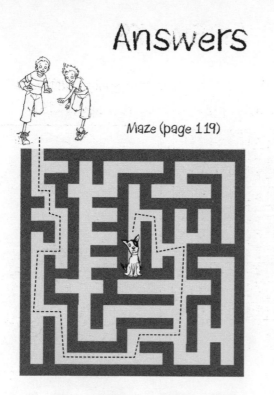

Are you a bug boffin?	Give yourself a point for every
(page 121)	question you got right.
Answer 1) B	6–8 POINTS — You are a real bug
Answer 2) A	boffin! Nothing gets past you.
Answer 3) C	3–5 POINTS — You are SWITCHed on!
Answer 4) B	You enjoy a good adventure.
Answer 5) A	0–2 POINTS — Oh dear, looks as if you
Answer 6) B	need to brush up on your bug skills!
Answer 7) A	Better luck next time!
Answer 8) B	

About the author

Ali Sparkes grew up in the woods of Hampshire.
Actually, strictly speaking she grew up in a house
in Hampshire. The woods were great but lacked
basic facilities like sofas and a well stocked fridge.
Nevertheless, the woods were where she and
her friends spent much of their time and so Ali
grew up with a deep and abiding love of wildlife.
If you ever see Ali with a large garden spider on
her shoulder she will most likely be screeching
'AAAAAAAAAARRRRRGHGETITOFFME!'

Ali lives in Southampton with her husband and sons
and would never kill a creepy-crawly of any kind. They
are more scared of her than she is of them. (Creepy-
crawlies, not her husband and sons.)

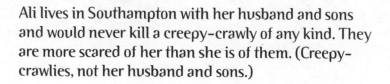

Other books
in the **SWITCH** series
SERUM WHICH INSTIGATES TOTAL CELLULAR HIJACK

SERUM WHICH INSTIGATES TOTAL CELLULAR HIJACK

Whether you're interested in insects
or terrified of tarantulas, you'll love the
S.W.I.T.C.H. website!

Find out more about the creatures in
Josh and Danny's adventures, enter fantastic
competitions, read the first chapters
of all of the S.W.I.T.C.H. books, and enjoy
creepy-crawly games and activities.

www.switch-books.co.uk